ALTA

A Valmenessian Novella

Rebecca Camm

Alta
Copyright © 2023 by Rebecca Camm
Revised Edition: August 2023

Find me at: www.rebeccacamm.com
Instagram: @readingwritingdaydreaming
TikTok: @readingwritingdaydream
Facebook: @readingwritingdaydreaming

Printed in Australia.

Paperback ISBN: 978-0-6453455-9-9

Editor; Chloe Hodge – chloehodge.com
Proof-reader & Editor; Emily Morrison – emilymorrisoneditorial.com
Cover Design & Formatter; Rebecca Camm – rebeccacamm.com

This book is written in British English

THE VALMENESSIAN CHRONICLES

Content Notes

Alta is an adult fantasy novella. It contains cursing, sexual references, violence, assault, and other adult themes.
A full list can be found on my website, rebeccacamm.com or by scanning the QR code below.

Valmenessia

The Frozen Sea

The Peraylum Mountains

The Great Northern Forest

Kalbom

Fenrick's Cliff

Fenton

Greenfield Woods

Milhelpum

Giland

Bowton

Dogbert Harbour

Fenkton

Royal Bay

Ocean's Harbour

Blessed Reef

Crssing

The Mines

Whitewater's Forest

Surfey

Sailor's Peril

The Dividing Waters

1

The cool sea breeze blew through the open window beside Nora, caressing her exposed stomach and providing little respite from the stifling heat within the corridor of the seaside townhouse. Glancing outside, Nora looked to the people bustling about below as they went about their business. Dockworkers helped unload cargo or the fishing catch of the day from ships, and stall owners sold their wares and others prepared food for those seeking something to fill their bellies. Potential customers either walked by swiftly to avoid the calls of those selling or stopped to make purchases and admire the view of the harbour itself. Nora looked to the waters beyond the street, the sun turning the sea bordering Ocean's Harbour into a glittering jewel. It was a pretty city, though Nora would not have time to explore it. She was here because she had a job to do.

Inside the townhouse, servants passed by unbothered by those waiting in line with Nora in the narrow corridor. Instead, they went about their duties cleaning or carrying supplies to wherever it was they were needed as though it were just another ordinary day, which Nora supposed for them it was. Sweat clung to Nora's skin as she neared the front of the line; she'd been waiting for at least a few hours now, dressed in an outfit that left very little to the imagination.

"I wish they would make their decisions quicker," Nora huffed under her breath. She folded her arms over her pale chest, accentuating the low cut of her top. It was made of a green tight-fitting fabric, which left her toned stomach and a decent amount of her cleavage on display, whilst covering her arms entirely. Tight leather pants clung to her lower half from hip to just above her ankles, and on her feet were strappy sandals. Nora had scoffed at the idea of wearing shorts, but as the sun was now at its peak, she was regretting that decision. Especially as the line was moving slower than a snail.

"Are you always so impatient?" the man behind her chuckled and, she glanced up at him, narrowing her gaze. He, too, was dressed in a way that exposed a lot of skin. He wore tight leather shorts with matching boots and his tanned chest was bare and oiled, accentuating his muscular build. If they'd been made to wait outside in the sun he would have cooked like the fish currently being fried on the streets below.

"More like I'm bored," she replied, flicking her chocolate brown hair over her shoulder so that the waves fell against her back. "I hate feeling idle."

"You should have seen the lines for Lord Porcella's son's eighteenth birthday a couple months ago," he said. His blue eyes sparkled much like the water beyond the window, and his lips tugged up at one side, clearly entertained by her mood. "Every pleasure worker within a week's journey was vying to be chosen for it."

Nora quirked a brow. "The tips were that good?"

"Uh-huh," the man said with a wink. "Invites went out to hundreds of influential people. There was a lot of coin passing hands that night."

Of course there was, Nora thought. The nobility in Royal Bay spared no expense, especially when it came to high profile events. There was no price they wouldn't pay if it meant gaining status or power. She doubted the nobility in Ocean's Harbour would be much different.

The man nudged her shoulder gently. "The line's moving."

"Keep your panties on," Nora said, batting his hand away before turning around.

Nora stepped forward, following the woman in front of her. The silk fabric clinging to her brown skin was more revealing than Nora's. Her golden eyes and pointed ears identified her as a Lys Alv, but not all races were so easy to pick. Unless they displayed their magic, Nora could only assume the others were human. There were five races in the country of Valmenessia: humans; Elementums that wielded fire, water and wind magic; Anima who shifted from human to an animal form; and then the Alvs with their pointed ears. The Alvs were split into two races: Lys Alvs with golden eyes and healing magic; and Mors Alvs with black eyes who were rumoured to steal health and magic. Under the king's orders, the latter were eradicated nearly twenty years ago in order to protect the populace.

A petite woman with black hair tied in a braid at the base of her neck and blood-red lips popped her head out of the far room, waving her bejewelled hand at those in the line. "He's ready to see the next five of you."

"Finally," Nora murmured under her breath.

She strode into the room and stood before a man with an oily smile and a fine suit. The Lys Alv stood on Nora's left and the man she'd been speaking to in the corridor was on her other side. Next to the Lys Alv was a woman with a button nose and a black bob, short as though cut with a single swipe of a sharp blade, then beside her was a tall man with cropped brown hair and dazzling green eyes. Unlike Nora, who was eyeing her competition, everyone else had their gazes forward, awaiting direction.

"Well, aren't you all delectable," the man in the suit leered, the tone of his voice making Nora's stomach curl. She hated people like that. Those who thought they could charm people into submission because they believed they owned the world. He plastered an exaggerated pout on his face. "We can't take you all."

"It is a pity, Jonathan," the petite woman who'd called them into the room said. Her gaze dragged over each of them as though they were a meal, and she was free to choose whichever she pleased to devour.

Jonathan ran the backs of his fingers down the arm of the Lys Alv and Nora saw the woman flinch in an almost imperceptible move. Nora usually didn't mind the kind of work she was hoping to obtain from this man, but the audition process she could do without. She had some choice words for Jonathan, who continued to peruse the six who stood before him as though choosing a pastry from a baker's store, but she kept her mouth shut. She needed this job if she had any chance of getting into Lord Porcella's exclusive Scorch Season celebration the following night.

After arriving in Ocean Harbour that morning, she'd quickly set about making her plans fall into place. King Dominic had commanded her to kill a man at Lord Porcella's celebration and, as it was an invitation-only event, posing as a pleasure worker had been the best way in. The intimacy this line of work required would bring her closer to her target than any other form of entertainer entering the lord's estate. Nora was eager to fulfil the king's wishes—the magical shackle tattoos that encircled her wrists urging her to succeed. The tattoos were what tied her to King Dominic and marked her as one of the Alta; something that Nora thought was the best thing to ever happen to her.

The Alta were King Dominic's secret soldiers. Strong magic wielders trained in combat, assassination, and other dangerous arts. Due to the tattoos, every Alta in his hidden army had the desire to follow the king's commands. King Dominic could have used his Royal Sentries to enforce his laws, but sometimes weeds needed to be removed swiftly and without notice. Digging up the plant could cause more damage than good, so here Nora was, weeding out those the king deemed a threat.

"So, who have we got here?" Jonathan asked, stepping in front of the man at the other end of the line. "What special talent do you have?"

"Jez," the man said, then gestured up and down his toned body. "And I'm the talent."

Jonathan smiled, though it didn't reach his eyes. "Cute, but everyone auditioning today is pretty on the eyes."

The man frowned, opening his mouth to reply, but Jonathan had already moved on to the woman beside him. "And you?"

"I'm Mable," she said with a small squeak. "And I can shift into an impala."

"Interesting," Jonathan replied, stroking his chin. "They're not native here." This time when he smiled, it was broad, though no less unnerving than the one he'd directed at Jez. "How very exotic."

Mable's cheeks flushed a rosy pink as Jonathan turned his attention to the Lys Alv. "What is your name, beautiful?"

"Belle."

"Now that's fitting," Jonathan chuckled. "What is your talent?"

Belle bit her lip. "My fast healing."

"Of course it is." Jonathan winked.

"How is that any different to what I said?" Jez asked irritably from down the line. He stepped forward, his hands on his hips and scoffed. "What use is healing in our line of work?"

"Her magic is invaluable for certain clientele," Jonathan scowled, raising his chin. "You are useless. Just a pretty shell with nothing more to offer. So here's some advice, free of charge.

Your life has no worth unless you have a skill. In this industry or any other. This country values what you can give it, and you have nothing to offer."

Jez clenched his fists and stormed forward, and Nora readied herself to summon magic. She may not have liked Jonathan, but he was her means to an end and she would not let Jez ruin things.

"Leave before you make a fool of yourself and ruin any chances of a career in this industry," Jonathan said calmly before Jez could reach him.

Jez's face reddened but he relented, marching out of the room and grumbling under his breath an impressive number of profanities.

"Now, where was I?" Jonathan asked cheerily as though the incident had never occurred. He clasped his hands behind his back and bounced on the balls of his feet.

"Me," Nora said, drawing her shoulders back. "I'm Nora. A friend in Royal Bay suggested I audition for you."

"Is that so?" His gaze dragged up and down her body like an unwanted caress. "And your talent?"

"Let me show you," she said, extending her hand.

Jonathan placed his hand in hers, intrigue dancing in his eyes. Nora gripped his wrist, then, with her other hand, pushed up the sleeve of his suit to expose his arm. She was an Elementum—a strong one at that with the ability to wield fire, water and wind equally—but for this little demonstration, all she needed was one. She summoned her fire magic, letting the flames lick over his skin with enough heat to tingle but not burn.

"Now that's a talent I could enjoy," Jonathan chuckled as she released him. "And maybe the day after Lord Porcella's celebration I will."

He winked at Nora, then moved to the man she'd been speaking to in the hallway. Nora held in her gag as she too focused her attention on the man beside her.

"We've met before," Jonathan said, pressing up on his toes

6

to get a better look at the man's face.

"Yes, I'm Cole," he replied, smiling broadly and revealing a dimple in his cheek. "I was at the eighteenth."

Jonathan looked him up and down, then matched his smile. "Of course, I remember now." He stepped back, taking them all in once more. "So much beauty in a single room. You're all in!"

Nora looked to Cole and couldn't help the smile gracing her lips. She loved when her plans fell into place.

"Lola will show you to your rooms," Jonathan said, pointing to the woman who had ushered them inside earlier. "You'll be provided meals and other basic necessities so long as you are in my employment."

Lola led them down the corridor towards an archway at the very end. Beyond was an expansive hall filled with places to sit and eat. "Women upstairs on the left, men upstairs on the right," she said, gesturing to the stairs at the back of the room as she spoke. "There is a communal bathing chamber downstairs. The staff will bring up water unless one of you is a powerful enough Elementum to fill the tubs. Other than that, feel free to mingle. The only rules are no tears, no jealousy, and no pregnancies."

With that, Lola took one long look at Cole, her gaze resting on his chest for a moment longer, then turned and strode back the way they had come. Nora noticed movement in one of the large windows to her right, spotting a familiar dark cloak before the owner disappeared.

"Wanna hang out?" Beside her, Cole leant up against the archway, his tousled toffee brown hair falling into his eyes as he tilted his head in her direction. His tall and broad form towered over her. "See if we can break any of the rules?"

"Nope," Nora replied, accentuating the pop of the 'p.' "I already have plans."

"Really?" he grinned, raising his brows. "Do I have a little competition?"

She laughed, clutching her stomach. Her plans had nothing

to do with meeting a prospective partner—even considering who she was meeting in any light beyond friendship was beyond revolting.

"What?" Cole asked, his smile faltering.

"Nothing," she said with a wave of her hand. She wiped a stray tear from her eye then turned, heading back through the corridor, but not before pausing to call over her shoulder, "Maybe we can see about breaking those rules later!"

2

Despite sundown approaching, the open market was bustling with citizens of Ocean Harbour in the streets below. Stall owners were preparing various meals—most containing seafood—or buying and selling goods brought in by the large ships currently docked. Lord Porcella's sentries patrolled the harbour, inspecting ships and questioning those on board.

"I assume you made the cut," a familiar voice said. Nora smirked at the familiar cloaked figure who appeared beside her.

"Of course," she replied, placing a hand over her chest in mock horror. "Did you expect anything less?"

August chuckled as he gripped her arm, steering her off the main street towards a quieter part of the harbour. He stopped amongst a collection of crates, and she sat on one, crossing her legs beneath her and facing her best friend. August and Nora had grown up together since she was only six years old. He was a year older than her, and they had instantly become friends, even ter he'd almost killed her. It helped that they were the only children training as Alta. The older soldiers had often picked on them when they were younger and standing up for each other had forged their bond. Nora felt it was the most important relationship in her life—going beyond the ties she felt to the king who'd seen her value and taken her in. August was her best friend and the only family she'd had for the past thirteen years.

Nora frowned at the shadows beneath August's hood. When they were outside of Alta quarters, August wore his charcoal cloak to hide his identity. If anyone were to see who he truly was, he'd be executed before she could do anything to stop it.

"Must be hot in that thing," she stated, her tone teasing. During the cooler months, the cloak wasn't much of an issue, but during the peak of Scorch Season, she could only imagine how sweaty he would be.

"The alternative would be quite the spectacle," he replied dryly with a shrug.

"It would definitely liven things up around here." She glanced around them. There was barely anyone around and those she spotted were in the distance busying themselves in the market or around the ships. "Are you sure we won't be overheard here? We're supposed to be discreet, remember?"

"You're doubting me?" he asked.

She knew he'd be rolling his dark eyes at her from beneath that cloak.

The need for stealth and caution had been ingrained in them from an early age. August was stealthier than anyone she'd ever known but it was still fun to tease him. "You're not exactly the sharpest blade in the armoury, so I have to check every now and again."

"And you're the biggest bitch this side of Midskopas," August chuckled, and Nora stuck her tongue out at him in reply.

"Maybe," she grinned mischievously. "But you're an ass so we make a good team. Have you learnt anything useful from your spying?"

"Our target is rather boring and predictable so far," August said, sitting opposite her and spreading his legs wide as if he were lounging on a throne. "His day is full of meetings, but I've heard nothing notable. Seems like your everyday businessperson to me. He's not a threat as far as I can see."

"Are you questioning our task?" she asked, narrowing her eyes at him.

"Of course not, the king has his reasons for what he's asked of us," he replied, resting his elbows on his knees. "I saw him shift into a sloth."

That revelation was unexpected. "Really?" Nora asked in surprise.

"Yeah, I almost gave my cover away I was laughing so hard," he chuckled.

Nora grinned broadly at the remark. Anima nobility tended to have shifts of the more regal kind, so a sloth was quite... different.

"I'll be monitoring him until I meet with you tomorrow night," August continued with a sigh. "Hopefully there are no more surprises that test my ability to be discreet."

"Fingers crossed," Nora agreed. "Seems it's all going to plan then."

"Yeah, everything is running smoothly. We'll be back in Royal Bay by the end of the week."

Nora smiled at the idea of returning home as she glanced out at the sea.

The king's castle was located on an island in Royal Bay and, whilst the Alta and their headquarters were a secret in Valmenessia, she would often sneak out to watch the waves roll in. There was something peaceful about the sound and the motion of the water. August often suggested that it called to her water magic, but she wasn't going to read into it too much. Sometimes things were just enjoyable and that was all there was to it. Not everything needed to be analysed.

The water lapped at a grand ship's hull as it docked, and Nora watched as the stall vendors bustled about in preparation for potential customers. The visitors to Valmenessia stepped from the vessel to explore the harbour and were instantly faced with explosions of fire, water, and wind magic. Shouts of mysteries and wonder sounded as merchants hawked their wares and encouraged onlookers to spend coin. Many of the people were easily drawn in by the display of magic and the appearance of the Lys Alvs and Anima, having come from other countries where such abilities were non-existent. As far as Nora was aware, Valmenessia was the only country with magic in the entire world. There was something special about being born onto this land. If anyone with magic were to board a ship to a foreign country, they would find themselves stripped of their magic completely, with no chance of it returning, even if they came back home. No one knew why magic only existed in Valmenessia, but that was how it had always been.

This was why it was rare for anyone other than humans born without magic to leave Valmenessia. The sacrifice was too great.

"Nothing else to report then?" she asked August, turning back to her best friend.

He shrugged his broad shoulders. "Not from my end. What about you?"

"Nothing yet, though I doubt I'll learn anything valuable until I get into Lord Porcella's estate," she said. "You should probably get back. Wouldn't want to miss all the riveting stalking."

August chuckled, rising to his feet and towering over her, blocking out the afternoon sun. Even if she were standing he would still be a good head or two taller than her. "I'll see you tomorrow. Don't have too much fun while I'm gone."

"Okay, Rana," Nora teased, rolling her eyes. August barked a laugh at the mention of the Alta leader. They were both orphans and Rana was the closest thing they had to a parent.

August departed on silent feet and Nora decided to head back to the townhouse, her growling stomach begging for the free meal Jonathan had promised.

As she walked back, the tourists from the ship moved through the market, mostly stopping at the stalls occupied by Elementum, Anima or Lys Alvs. The Elementums continued to make a spectacle of their magic, whilst some Anima shifted back and forth between their animal and human forms, much to the delight of the new arrivals. A woman with golden eyes and pointed ears strode through the growing crowd, earning stares and whispers as she offered healing bracelets supposedly infused with her magic for a rather hefty sum of coin. Many took her up on the offer, eager to experience some sort of magic, even if what they were really getting was a pretty little lie. Lys Alvs were unable to make magical relics. The only people capable of such tasks were Conjurers—humans who could manipulate magic after many years of studying and perfecting their craft— and they were rare.

When she reached the townhouse, Nora made her way back to the back of the house where Jonathan had allocated them and found Cole. He was lounging on one of the sofas with a plate piled high with food resting on his bare chest. He'd changed his pants to looser fitting ones but clearly hadn't seen a need to put a shirt on. Nora strode over to him, and his eyebrows rose just as he was dangling a piece of smoked meat over his mouth.

"Enjoying yourself?" she asked, her lips tugging to one side. She stole a piece of cheese from his plate, popping it into her mouth.

"More now that you are here." He grinned and moved to sit up, patting the spot beside him. Nora took his offer, dropping onto the cushions. "Hungry?"

"Starving," she said, helping herself to more of his food.

Cole chuckled. "How'd your plans go?"

"Fine," Nora replied around a mouthful of herb bread. It was freshly baked, still warm in the middle, and tasted so good that she moaned.

"Judging by that little noise, I'm guessing you like the bread."

"An astute observation," she said sarcastically, glancing up at him.

Cole's eyes locked with hers, the corners of his lids creasing with amusement. "I bet there is something I can do that will put that bread to shame."

"Get me some more bread and I'll let you try your best," Nora said with a wink, her cheeks bulging with food.

With a grin, Cole handed her the plate and went to find her some more bread. With Cole gone, Nora observed the others in the room. Jonathan had finished recruiting workers for Lord Porcella's celebration and now they were all lounging around the room. Some were conversing over food, others relaxed on large cushions in the dwindling sunlight. There were even noises coming from above that suggested some were practising their craft. Nora ignored the sounds as she ate and waited for Cole.

"Here you are," he said upon his return. He carried a tray stacked with bread and, judging by the annoyed glances coming from a few people behind him, he had procured the entire supply.

"You didn't have to bring *all* the bread," she said with a laugh, reaching out for the tray eagerly. "Looks like you pissed a few people off."

"You never specified an amount, and I can't have you low on energy for what I have planned," he winked, making Nora's stomach flip. "I also brought this."

He pulled a bottle of wine from behind him, showing Nora before taking a long drink.

"How were you carrying that?" she asked, eyebrows raised. "Between your ass cheeks?"

Cole grinned. "A magician never reveals his secrets."

Nora stuffed more bread into her mouth, chewing slowly as Cole watched her intently, drinking his ass wine. They were both unashamedly admiring each other. His gaze slowly swept up and down her body as she took in his. He was tall, muscular, with toffee coloured hair, bright blue eyes rimmed with long lashes, and a strong jaw with the lightest brush of stubble.

"Ready?" Cole asked as she swallowed her last mouthful, offering his hand.

"Maybe we should have dessert?"

Cole lunged forward, picking her up and throwing her over his shoulder. Nora squealed, laughing as he carried her upstairs to one of the rooms.

"I'll be your dessert," he said, kicking the door shut behind them. Throwing her onto the bed, he grinned down at her, licking his lower lip, and Nora found herself clenching her thighs in anticipation. "I want you to do that fire thing to me that you did to Jonathan."

Nora traced her fingers over the hem of her pants. "Oh yeah? And what magic will you do for me?"

"I'm human," he replied, dropping his pants to reveal himself to her. "But I'm assuming this will make up for it."

"It's adequate," she replied haughtily, taking him in.

Completely naked, Cole strode towards her and gripped her pants, drawing them down her legs. Nora lifted her ass to help him and soon her lower half was completely bare. His gaze heated as he took in her nakedness, then he gripped both of her ankles in his strong hands. Nora yelped as he tugged her towards him, her ass almost falling off the edge of the bed.

"You're beyond adequate," Cole said, his voice deep with desire.

Nora sat up and angled her head towards him. "Kiss me."

He didn't hesitate, pressing his lips to hers. Cole sat beside her then drew her onto his lap as the kiss deepened. She straddled him, letting her hands explore his shoulders and chest, whilst he gripped her ass tightly. Nora made to reach between them, but Cole beat her to it, his hand slipping between her legs. She gasped, their kiss growing more intense as Cole continued teasing between her thighs.

'Please,' Nora panted against his mouth, grinding herself on his hand.

"What lovely manners," Cole replied huskily, biting Nora's bottom lip.

He slipped his fingers inside her and Nora tilted her head back, moaning, his fingers moving purposely. There was no hesitation in Cole's touch, speaking of his experience. Each thrust of his fingers inside her was measured, drawing out her pleasure.

Cole's pace quickened and Nora found herself holding onto him, her nails digging into his skin. She cried out, her orgasm rippling through her in a current of euphoria. He continued to fuck her with his hand until she fell onto his chest, panting heavily. Nora angled her head, placing hungry kisses up his neck and towards his jaw until she captured his lips once more. Cole moved beneath her, and Nora looked down, licking her lips at the sight of his arousal. Wrapping a hand around the base of him, she began to lower herself, but Cole gripped her hips, halting her movement.

Nora pouted, earning a smirk from him. He flipped them over, pressing her back into the bed and bracing his hands on either side of her head before pushing inside her. Nora summoned her fire magic, letting the flames dance along his skin. Cole moaned at the sensation, his head falling forward as his movements became faster and more frenzied.

Nora's back arched as her release shuddered through her and, Cole soon followed, moaning as he, too, came. Panting, he relaxed, pressing his chest to hers.

Nora made to speak but Cole pressed a finger to her lips. "Before you say anything, the night is young, and this is just a short break."

"Okay," she laughed. "But I have a favour to ask and I'm also going to need some of that ass wine."

3

N ora flicked her wrist, her wind magic whirling towards
August and causing his feet to slip from under him.

"Fuck!" he grunted as he thudded to the dusty
ground. "I thought we weren't using magic?"

Nora shrugged and wiped the sweat from her brow with the
back of her tattooed wrist. "It was an accident."

"Sure," August replied, rolling his eyes as he got to his feet
once more. "Maybe you should take extra lessons with Rana to
learn to control your magic better?"

"I can control my magic just fine," she retorted, a hand
moving to her hip whilst the other clutched the short sword
tighter.

"Not if you're unintentionally throwing gusts of wind around
the place," he said, then quirked a brow at her. "Unless you
were lying about that?"

Nora stuck out her tongue. There was no point in defending
herself. They both knew she was lying. Instead, she spun her

wrist, twirling her sword in her hand before launching an attack once more. August didn't hesitate, moving to counter her, their short swords clanging as they fought. She'd only used magic because August had been winning. He was stronger than her and more skilled in swordplay. She'd never admit it—especially not to him—but she wasn't stupid enough to lie to herself. That would be a quick way to get herself killed.

The sound of heavy breathing and metal hitting metal filled the space until August pressed his advantage and disarmed her.

"You lose," August smirked down at her, holding both blades to her throat.

"Only because I'm handicapped," she replied, using her finger to push them away.

The short swords were only used for training so Nora wasn't concerned about cutting herself, not that she would have been if the blades were sharp. She was used to being injured in her line of work and when they were Lys Alvs readily available for healing. Having Lys Alv Healers at their beck and call took away any hesitation about being injured. Though, even when Nora was away from Royal Bay and the easily accessible Healers, she wasn't too concerned about a few cuts here and there. She had almost as many scars on her body as she'd had wounds healed.

August chuckled, striding away from her to place both weapons on the rack on the wall. "Always making excuses."

Nora sat on the floor and sighed, falling onto her back and staring up at the stone ceiling of the expansive room. The training room was located below ground like the rest of the Alta quarters. It had no decoration other than the natural patterns of dark stone illuminated by the sconces lining the walls. Just like the Alta, their base was a secret too, not that anyone would ever come looking for it. Only select people were allowed on the island that housed the royal castle, let alone beneath it. When Nora was young, she'd felt that the dark rooms and hallways were eerie—the prospect of living underground something from a frightening tale—but she'd eventually grown used to it. Now she quite liked the idea of living right under everyone's noses, especially the most powerful in the country.

Placing a hand on her chest, she felt her body rise and fall as she caught her breath. August lay down next to her and she turned her head to see him sling an arm over his eyes as he, too, steadied his breathing.

"Next time, let's train with magic and see who comes out the winner," Nora suggested, grinning mischievously, nudging his side with her elbow. "I'm sure you won't be a cocky asshole then."

"Are you forgetting that I have magic too?" he asked without moving to look at her, completely ignoring the jabs in his side.

"Of course not," she laughed. "But it's not exactly a threat, is it?"

August opened his mouth to rebuke her teasing but was interrupted by Rana's voice. Nora looked over to see the woman standing in the doorway looking as striking as ever with her golden hair, soft features, and deep brown eyes. If she'd been wearing a ball gown instead of her Alta uniform she would have easily fit in amongst Royal Bay's most elite.

"You two, my office now," the leader of the Alta said, turning away and striding from the room as quietly as she had entered it.

Nora and August didn't need to be told twice, moving swiftly to their feet and heading after Rana. King Dominic was waiting in her office and, they quickly stood before their king, bowing in respect before looking to the man that commanded their fates.

King Dominic braced his elbows on the arms of Rana's desk, steepling his fingers to his lips as he leaned forward in his seat. His hazel eyes were analysing as he stared between the two of them, assessing and looking for any weaknesses. They had been instructed to the point that their training sessions were a form of devotion—a dance of their craft. Despite the time and effort she put in, when Nora stood before her king she felt as though he would be left wanting ... that she could be better.

"Rana will outline the job I want completed," he said, breaking the tense silence, his deep voice leaving no room for negotiation. "You will listen carefully to every detail, and you will be successful, otherwise you'll find yourselves in Goddess Jord's embrace."

Nora's tattoos hummed with each word that left his lips. The threat of the Mors Alv Goddess only added weight to his words. The Goddess Jord only appeared to escort one to the afterlife.

"Understood, my king," Nora and August spoke in unison, lowering their heads.

They waited with downcast eyes until King Dominic left the room. Once he'd departed, Nora lifted her chin to see Rana sitting in the vacant spot the king had left. The woman was one of the strongest Elementum in the country, and yet due to her position, no one other than the king and the Alta would know of her power.

"Your job"—Rana began, all business as she gathered papers from her desk and turned them to face Nora and August— "Is to eliminate a threat and bring Lord Porcella to the king's side."

Nora looked at Rana's desk to find a drawing of a man with deep brown eyes and a square jaw. His curly blond hair fell in ringlets around his face like a halo of sorts and a smattering of freckles sat over his broad nose and cheeks. A white line sliced through his right brow, reminding Nora of the scar that sat high on her cheek.

"Robert Swiften is the eldest son of one of the wealthiest noble Anima families in Ocean's Harbour. He's been organising passage for convicted criminals to leave the country, believing them wrongly imprisoned," Rana continued, reclining in her seat. "The king wants the Anima eliminated. Flaunting the breaking of laws is one thing, but Robert Swiften's actions encourage rebellion. He is a threat to the peace."

Nora nodded in understanding. She would not let anyone jeopardise the peace her king had created in Valmenessia.

"Lord Porcella has been sympathetic to Robert Swiften's cause even though it goes against the king's laws," Rana said her gaze flicking between Nora and August. "But King Dominic is willing to give the Elementum lord another chance."

"How are we supposed to persuade Lord Porcella to fall in line then?" Nora asked, running a finger over the edge of the sketch of Robert Swiften.

"Among certain circles, Robert Swiften is seen as a sort of hero from children's tales who helps those in need. His actions, if left unattended, are a disease that would spread and cause unrest amongst the people. He is a threat to our very way of life and everything, we as Alta, strive to protect."

"So we kill him," August stated matter of factly. "Erase him from the story."

"Correct," Rana nodded. "Though we are going to use his death not only to eliminate a threat but bring Lord Porcella in line. You are to kill Robert Swiften in a manner that would frame the lord. Once he is panicked and faced with the prospect of his people's anger, offer King Dominic's assistance to clear the matter up. King Dominic will stand by Lord Porcella and protect him from any backlash from the nobles in his city. All the lord must do in return is follow this story and send his son to Royal Bay as a show of good faith."

"It all seems very convoluted," Nora said, glancing sidelong at August.

"Politics is often referred to as a game of chess but it's more like a spider's web," Rana said. "Stringing webs in patterns from trusted points until one day, the prey flies too close and is caught in the net of all that careful planning. Lord Porcella has been avoiding King Dominic's web for years, refusing to enforce laws just to line his pockets with coin. It's now time for his disobedience to come to an end and remember who it is he *answers to. You will bring Lord Porcella's son back to Royal Bay so the next generation of Elementum lords in the harbour city will not make the same errors in judgment."*

August stepped forward, gathering the assorted intel on Robert Swiften. "And the story we give Lord Porcella to convince the people?"

"A version of the truth," Rana replied calmly. "That Robert Swiften is a traitor to the king and country. That he is exploiting the vulnerable, taking their hard-earned coin and sending them across the waters under the guise of freeing the unfairly persecuted."

"The people will then praise Lord Porcella and King Dominic for protecting them," Nora grinned. She loved enforcing King Dominic's will. She was the hand that herded the unwitting into the king's web where, just like a spider, he lay in wait without having to reveal himself.

Rana nodded then opened her drawer and retrieved a metal tube. "Give this to Lord Porcella once he's agreed to the terms."

"What's in there?" Nora asked, taking the tube.

"Exactly what Lord Porcella needs to solidify his story," Rana replied, rising from her seat. "Now, Lord Porcella's private Scorch Season celebration takes place at the end of the week and there will be many high-ranking guests attending. Seems like the perfect opportunity to set his lordship on the right track. Nothing like a potential audience to spur things in motion."

"And how will we get an invite to this exclusive event?"

Rana pointed to the stack of papers August held. "Find Jonathan. For the right face and skillset, he won't bother with a background check."

Nora awoke with Cole sprawled out on his front beside her and the memory of King Dominic and Rana's orders on her mind. Without waking her companion, she climbed out of bed, taking the thin sheet with her and leaving Cole bare. She made her way to the window, sliding it open to let in the fresh air. The scent of the ocean instantly twirled through the opening, embracing Nora.

Music and the commotion of a crowd tumbled in after the breeze, and Nora stuck her head out to see if she could witness where the noise was coming from. Unable to find the source, she hastily retrieved her clothing, dressed quickly, then climbed out the window. Using her wind magic to give her extra support she used the window frame and the cracks in the stone building to climb up the wall and onto the rooftop. The tiles were hot beneath her feet, but she didn't let it bother her as she crept towards a section shaded by the taller building next door. Sitting in the shade, she was now in prime position to watch as the commotion drew nearer.

Lord Porcella's private celebration may have been set to begin that evening, but his public festivities were in full swing. A parade made its way through the streets, much to the delight of the citizens who came out from their homes and workplaces to watch. Elementum used their magic to summon spectacles of fire and water magic, whilst dancers in hues of orange, yellow and red spun through the streets. Drummers beat their instruments as they danced to the rhythm they were creating, and behind them all, was an open-top carriage pulled by two caramel brown horses. Lord Porcella sat waving at the people, a broad smile plastered on his face.

The crowds cheered for their lord and Nora felt her confidence grow. The people loved him, and even though they may not like the story he would have to tell them, they would trust him. Rana had said Robert Swiften was a man of the people, but judging by this display, Lord Porcella was too.

Twirling her hair through her fingers, Nora contemplated the day ahead.

All her and August's carefully laid plans would come together over the next few hours. Excitement danced in her veins as though her fire magic had sparked beneath her skin. She loved the time before she made to strike, the anticipation fuelling her determination. King Dominic had given his commands, and she was yet to let him down. Tonight would be no exception; she and August would succeed.

4

Groomed horses and glossy carriages lined the wide gravel path that led to the mansion's entrance, each more extravagant than the next as though they were all competing in some sort of ostentatious competition. To some degree they were; nobles were always trying to outdo each other. Nora ignored the carriages, her attention on the horses as she admired their beauty. She had a fondness for animals, true animals that is, and horses were one of her favourites. Horses were always good judges of character.

Stones crunched beneath her feet as she continued onto the buffed stone steps and into the manor. Stepping through the towering double doors, Nora admired the Scorch Season decorations. Ribbons in bright yellows, oranges, and reds hung from the tall ceiling, cascading down in waves. Floral arrangements in similar colours lined the walls, reminding Nora of the sun shining brightly in the sky. The smell of sweet and spicy food mixed with the sea air, and Nora inhaled deeply, her stomach growling as she hoped to taste what was being prepared in the kitchens.

Nora glimpsed inside an expansive hall where nobles dressed in their finery mingled in groups, laughing and talking as trays of food and wine were offered by passing servants. On small stages throughout, entertainers performed in displays of sleight of hand, magic, art, music or dance. Nora didn't know what to focus on as her gaze flitted between the intriguing performances, not that she was given much of a chance to look. Lord Porcella's staff ushered her and the rest of Jonathan's workers away from the festivities and the sight of the guests.

Cole walked by Nora's side and, after spending the night together, they hadn't managed to break any of Jonathan's rules. He offered her a warm smile, giving her shoulder a reassuring squeeze. Part of her wished she could take him back to Royal Bay with her, not for a relationship or even friendship for that matter, but to repeat their fun from the night before. With a sigh, she pushed the thought away. After tonight, he would see her in a different light.

They strode through Lord Porcella's grand home along with the other courtesans who had been hired by Jonathan for the festivities. Nora was dressed in amber silk that wrapped around her chest and matching flowing skirt with a slit up the side that exposed her thigh when she walked. Kohl lined her eyes and a bright red balm had been applied to her lips to draw the eye. Nora had also stolen a simple make-up one of the ladies had made from ingredients borrowed from the kitchens and covered the tattoos around her wrists, obscuring the king's claim. Not that their meaning was common knowledge, but it was better to hide them than be seen by someone who was privy to classified information.

The women were all dressed similarly, only in varying shades of yellow and orange, and the men wore tight-fitting trousers in the array of colours, their torsos bare. They were all led onto the second floor and into a room filled with lush seating and hidden alcoves. Large windows on the far walls provided a beautiful view of the harbour and the sunset beyond, letting in a gentle sea breeze.

"The guests will be arriving shortly," Jonathan said, stuffing his hands into his suit pockets. Nora could only imagine how disgusting and sweaty his shirt would be under his suit jacket with the day still being so warm. "I want you all looking relaxed and inviting when they arrive. I have a reputation to uphold."

Everyone moved to make themselves comfortable, some tending to their appearances whilst others began consuming the sparkling wine in earnest. One of the Anima men shifted into a black panther before lounging on a sofa and letting out a feline yawn. Nora found a place to stand, and it wasn't long before the festivities were brought upstairs. Up close, Nora was able to appreciate the details of the guests' outfits; the gold and silver buttons and buckles, the shimmering jewels hanging from necks, wrists and ears. Nora moved through the people, smiling demurely and ignoring suggestive touches as she scanned the room for Robert Swiften, the man Rana had set as their target. Music played as waiters carrying trays lined with glasses of sparkling alcohol and bite-sized food circled the room.

Guests and courtesans mingled, some even dancing in the centre of the room. She glanced over to Cole where he stood between a man and a woman who were both running their hands up and down his chest. Neither was looking at him, too engrossed in their conversation to acknowledge the person they were feeling up. Cole sensed her gaze and quirked a smile at her which she answered by quickly sticking her tongue out at him just as the music ceased and the conversation hushed.

Nora turned her attention to where a stocky man with greying hair and a confident smile stood near the door. He wore a white shirt with gold patterns threaded through the fabric and loose pants in hues of burnt orange. Lord Porcella took in the room, his rich brown eyes trailing over his guests. Up close, he was more captivating than he had been in the parade earlier that day. Nora could see why the people were drawn to him and judging by the expressions of the nobles around her, they were just as in love with the man as the commoners.

How loved could Robert Swiften possibly be that his death could turn all these people against the lord? Nora wondered, chewing her lip.

"Let the fun continue my friends!" He exclaimed, saluting those present with a wine glass held in his brown hand. The liquid rose from the glass, swirling in the air above it in a dance. The guests cheered at what Nora would have described as a pathetic demonstration of magic. The wine dropped back into the glass and Lord Porcella saluted those gathered once more before moving to join a conversation nearby.

The music started up again and Nora circled the perimeter, glancing into alcoves that were already occupied and snagging a few mini cakes from a passing server. She stuffed her face, savouring the sweet taste on her tongue. A moan escaped her, which garnered attention from a group nearby, but she quickly slipped away, not wanting to be caught up with anyone while she searched for Robert Swiften. As her eyes scanned the crowd for her target, she tuned in to snippets of confirmation, listening for anything of note.

"The fabric is a silk from the southern continent," one woman said, gesturing to her gown as Nora passed. "I don't usually purchase from an Anima, but it was too fine to pass up. I had my lady in waiting wash it three times before I wore it tonight, just in case."

Another standing in a small group tugged a lock of hair behind her ear as she spoke to her companion. "The Anima was arrested for brutality, but that is to be expected of their kind."

"Indeed. They're becoming quite the issue." Her companion replied.

Nora hadn't heard of the Anima being a wider issue, but she was sure that if there was a problem King Dominic would do something to protect the people. The king was always striving to keep order and peace. She crossed to the other side of the room, only slowing to overhear another conversation.

"Lord Haaken is a pain in my side," the man in front of her commented gruffly as those beside him nodded in agreement. "He's making it harder for my traders to sell in his city. Something about uncertainty in the times ahead."

"The man is mad to think his people can be self-sufficient from the rest of the country," the person beside him said, stuffing his hands into his pockets. "And his insanity is messing with our bottom lines. I'll bring it up with Lord Porcella at the next meeting."

Nora rolled her eyes. Lord Haaken in Sorby was renowned for protecting his human-only population from the rest of the country. The king gave him leeway to put extra restrictions on those who entered his city purely because the lord remained neutral and followed the laws. If Lord Haaken didn't want Lord Porcella's citizens trading in Sorby then Lord Porcella had no power. King Dominic would not be stepping in, especially when Lord Porcella was behaving like a disobedient child.

Moving past the grumpy business people, Nora's gaze caught on the man she'd been looking for. He ran a hand through his curly blond hair as he spoke to the rather large group gathered around him. His audience was smiling and laughing, their attention caught on his every word. Nora did a quick scan of the windows that were now opened to the dark sky. If Robert was here then so was August, though the likelihood of spotting her best friend when he purposely didn't want to be seen was impossible. He wouldn't make himself known until he wanted.

Looking back to where Robert Swiften stood, Nora smiled and headed towards him. Just as she was about to reach him, someone caught hold of her arm and spun her around.

"Come have a drink with me," the man holding her said, a playful smile gracing his face.

Fuck, she was tempted. The man was around her age; average height, with tanned skin, chiselled features, and captivating dark brown eyes. Nora chewed her lip, contemplating agreeing, but then her wrists started to itch, reminding her of the task at hand. She had to deal with Robert Swiften first.

"Maybe later," she said, batting her eyelashes at the man who'd propositioned her. If she could deal with the task set for her quickly, she might have be able to make time for a little bit of fun.

"Why not now?" he asked, tilting his head to one side and looking all kinds of adorable. He knew how to play the game and she couldn't deny that it was working.

"I have someone else to go to first,' she replied, unable to hide the disappointment in her voice.

The man released her as though stung, his face twisting in disgust. "I don't want anyone's seconds."

Nora fought to keep her face neutral even though she wanted to sneer at this man and possibly slap him too. He'd gone from swoon-worthy to jerk in less time than it took to blink. He'd deserve more than a slap with his insinuation that her value lay in being untouched. What a fucking asshole.

"Your loss," Nora replied with a smile that she was sure as shit knew looked sarcastic. She turned away from the man, searching once more for Robert Swiften, only to see that he was no longer anywhere in sight.

5

Hiding in one of the alcoves, Nora monitored the crowd beyond the sheer curtains for any sign of her target. Annoyingly, she couldn't spot him amongst the sea of bodies, but even more frustrating was the fact that August still hadn't made himself known either. She'd seen Robert in the room so August should have been lurking in the shadows somewhere too, seeing as he was stalking the man. She wanted to check in with her friend and it pissed her off that he was still concealing himself from her.

On the bright side, the rude man she'd encountered earlier that evening had stayed over the other side of the room, occupied by someone else he must have deemed pure enough for his standards. The festivities were now becoming more debauch, the wine and darkening hour showing the nobles' true colours. Guests were slipping away with courtesans; others were deep in discussions or sitting around tables playing card games. Nora liked watching the nobles let their hair down. It was at times like this when they were no different than everyone else. Sure, they had nicer clothing and wine, but their desires were all the same.

Sipping the last of the sparkling wine from her glass and placing it on the small table beside her, Nora pursed her lips. She'd have to go back into the festivities soon. She'd held off several guests trying to claim the alcove from her—among other things—but soon her feigned illness would no longer stop anyone from calling her out.

Nora had smudged the makeup on her wrists, contemplating the dark ink that was tattooed in an intricate design on her pale skin. They were beautiful. Made up of swirls and loops—a complete contrast to their name. The Alta referred to them as shackle tattoos as they bound the wearer to King Dominic, but they appeared nothing of the sort. At least on the outside. The magic that ran through them, however, was much stronger than any metal and infinitely more binding.

"Robbie! You're walking too fast; I can't keep up in these shoes! Robbie!"

Robert Swiften hastily strode past her alcove, catching her interest through the sheer curtains. She flicked her wrist, causing him to trip over his feet. Robert Swiften landed on the tiled floor with a smack, those around him barely escaping falling with him as he flung his hands out. Nora's eyes widened, a little shocked at what she'd caused. She hadn't meant for the wind to be so strong. Quickly, she darted to his side, schooling her expression to one of concern.

"Are you okay?" Nora asked, pinching her brows as she placed her hand on Robert's shoulder.

"Oh Robbie!" A woman called, dropping beside Nora. "I told you to slow down!"

"I'm fine," Robert replied gruffly, rising to his feet, his face reddened, hiding the freckles over his nose and cheeks. He didn't move to push Nora's hand away though, so she ran it down his arm in a smooth caress.

The woman noticed the gesture, her eyes narrowing at where Nora's hand now rested on Robert's arm. "Come Robbie, you should sit."

"I—ah—"

"She's right," Nora said sweetly, indicating to the alcove beside them. "Come sit with me."

"I don't think your presence is necessary," the woman pursed her lips.

"Actually, I think I will sit with her," Robert said, sounding relieved as he adjusted his shirt before fidgeting with the collar, and following her into the secluded space. Through the sheer curtain, Nora watched as the woman stamped her foot, shooting Nora a venomous look before stomping away.

"Thank you," he said, sitting down on the cushioned seat beside her, his thigh pressing against her own. He ran a hand through his hair. "She's been following me all night."

"My pleasure." Nora turned her body towards him, placing her hand on his chest and toying with the silver buttons. "After all I'm here to please the guests of Lord Porcella."

Robert's gaze dropped to where her hand lay then drifted up her arm before looking her over, as if only now recognising how she was dressed. Nora bit her lower lip, letting her hand follow the trail of buttons down his front. He caught her wrist, holding her at his shiny buckle. For a minute, Nora thought he was going to reject her advances. It'd be just her luck that her target wasn't like the other guests in the room who enjoyed the bodies of those paid to entertain them. Holding still, she looked up at him through her lashes and held his gaze. The tension in the alcove thickened as Nora waited for him to make the next move and prayed to the Elementum Goddess, Thyra, to help her cause.

"Or maybe mine?" he said in a husky tone, proving that he was exactly like the rest of Lord Porcella's guests. Releasing her hand, he reached up to cup her face in his calloused fingers. "Falling over may have been a strange stroke of luck."

He pulled her to him, his lips clashing with hers in a bruising kiss. It wasn't pleasant, but Nora had learnt over the years that powerful people only cared about their own pleasures. Robert forced her mouth open with his tongue, and she endured one of the worst kisses of her life as she was bombarded with a tongue that would have rivalled the movement of the fish that landed on the ships docked in the harbour. She didn't push him away, and it only made to spur his confidence because soon his hands were everywhere, and Nora had to fight the urge to bat him away.

Instead, she broke the kiss, looking into his desire-filled eyes. "Shall we go somewhere more private?"

"Is this not private enough for you?" he asked breathlessly, his hands still moving all over her body, exploring her bare skin and curves.

"To a point," she replied, trying to sound sultry. "If you want to make things a little more fun…"

He grinned at her, licking his lips. "Lead the way."

Nora stood, the movement more abrupt than she'd planned and took his hand in hers. She led him through the crowd and out into the hallway in search of Lord Porcella's office. She opened a few doors, making excuses as to why they were not suitable before opening a glossy wooden door and finding the office. Within the space, the walls were lined from floor to ceiling with leather-bound books and expensive looking artefacts, and at the centre of the room were neatly stacked papers on top of a large wooden desk with a patterned rug beneath it.

She tugged Robert into the office, and he eagerly followed, shutting the door behind them. He immediately moved to embrace her, roughly pushing her up against the desk in his haste. His lips returned to hers in a one-sided frenzy as Nora lifted herself to sit on the desk to stop her ass from bruising against the angled edge of the desk. He mistook the action as enthusiasm and slid into the space between her legs without hesitation, pushing up against her so she could feel his arousal.

Before his eagerness could go any further Nora broke the kiss and quickly placed her hand over his mouth, summoning her water magic. Robert tried to pull back, his eyes wide in surprise but she wrapped her legs around his waist and her free arm circled his neck, pulling him close.

Robert's fingers dug into her flesh as he tried to pry her from him, then he shoved her chest with a force she hadn't expected. Nora fell backwards over the desk, tumbling over the top and scattering the neat stacks of paper all over the floor. Quickly jumping to her feet, her body aching the assault, she narrowed her eyes on where Robert stood, his hands on his thighs as he gasped for air.

"Please! Wait!" He cried out. "I'm not who you think I am!"

Nora ignored him, his words no doubt the desperate lies of a man who knew he was going to die. She summoned her water magic again, throwing a jet at him and silencing his pathetic pleas. He slammed against the wall, and she leapt for him. Wrapping her arms, neck and, legs around his torso, locking his arms at his sides, she slammed a hand over his mouth once more. She forced water down his throat and pinched his nose for good measure. Gargled noises escaped his mouth as the water overflowed and ran down his front, wetting them both. He fought her, spinning them around and slamming her back into the wall repeatedly. Nora groaned, a hanging sculpture cutting into her back. She loosened her grip as she felt the warmth of her blood spill down her back, and that was all it took. He threw her off him, lunging on top of her and holding her down on the ground.

She growled in anger, fighting against where his hands held her wrists, just as the door creaked open.

Fuck, she thought snapping her brown eyes to the doorway over Robert's shoulder, but then August appeared. She'd recognise his build in that dark cloak anywhere. He looked like a servant of the Goddess Jord, come to escort them to the afterlife. August strode up behind Robert, casual as fuck and put a dagger in his back. Repeatedly.

Robert gasped; his eyes as wide as the Scorch Season sun in his surprise before he collapsed onto Nora's chest. She grunted at the impact, supporting his weight as August continued. Blood spurted from the wound in Robert's back, splattering Nora with each stab. She felt the moment his life ceased; his life had been taken before he could grasp what was happening. August, with the tip of his boot, kicked Robert off Nora.

"I was trying not to make a mess," Nora said, gesturing to where blood pooled around Robert and was flicked onto the walls and furniture close by. Finally, she waved a hand down her front; her outfit was ruined, and she could feel the blood that speckled her face.

"Oh, I'm sorry," August replied, gesturing around the room where the papers were scattered, and water dripped from the shelves. "I can see you were being very conscious of keeping the place neat and tidy."

She rolled her eyes, accepting his hand as he helped her to her feet. "I was using my water magic to make it look like Lord Porcella was responsible."

"Well, maybe he likes to use daggers as well as magic," he suggested, shrugging his shoulders before wiping his blade on the dead man's clothes and hiding it back in his boot. If only Nora had been able to wear her boots, then maybe she, too, could have killed Robert with a weapon. "Look, the mess is not the problem."

"What do you mean?" she asked, tilting her head to one side and folding her arms over her chest.

"That wasn't Robert Swiften."

Nora pointed to where the man lay on the floor. "Look at him! That is Robert Swiften."

August shook his head. "No, that's a decoy. A Conjurer altered his appearance and then they sent him here. Robert Swiften knew someone was after him."

"Fuck!" Nora growled, stamping her foot in frustration. Altering someone's appearance was difficult magic for a Conjurer. There were limits; a person's race couldn't be hidden. Lys Alvs and Mors Alvs would still have their distinctive eyes and ears, even if the rest of them appeared as someone from another race. "Where is the *real* Robert Swiften?"

"At his home," August replied. While Nora's job had been to secure a position with Jonathon, August had been monitoring Robert's every move. They hadn't bothered to keep such a close eye on Lord Porcella, the man lived his life in the spotlight, so his movements were known to all. "The man is paranoid and as far as I could tell, no one but the Conjurer and this dead man knew of his plans."

"Shit," she said, pacing back and forth. "We can still make this work."

"What's the plan?"

Nora looked up at his hooded form. "Threaten to pin the murder of this man on the lord. He doesn't know it's not the real Robert Swiften. Once we have him agree to our demands, we find the real Robert Swiften and kill him."

"Right," August nodded, placing his hands on his hips. The movement drew the front of his cloak open to reveal his sleek black uniform beneath. "You might want to clean yourself up if you plan to entice the lord to come here with you."

"I'm not going anywhere," she smiled mischievously. "He will be here very soon and, when he arrives, there is something I'll need you to do."

6

Nora sat on the desk, picking at her nails as they waited. She'd wiped the blood from her face and any other bare skin, but there was nothing she could do about her stained clothing. She might be able to pass it as some sort of pattern on her clothing; it was night now, but anyone who got too close would know the crimson stain for what it truly was. The fake Robert Swiften still lay on the floor where August had rolled him off Nora, blood no longer leaking from his still chest. His eyes were wide open, staring into nothing, and Nora did her best to avoid looking at him. It wasn't that she felt bad about what she'd done, she just hated the vacant look of the dead. There was something unnerving about the way their eyes no longer glistened. Usually, she would close them, but they'd decided against it. The sight would be more impactful on Lord Porcella and hopefully, help to persuade him to do the right thing.

"How do you know Lord Porcella will come?" August asked, pulling tight the strip of fabric they were using as a bandage and earning a yelp from Nora.

He'd been tending to the wound she received when the fake Robert Swiften had shoved her against the hook on the wall. It wasn't life-threatening, but August had insisted on bandaging it up in case it started to bleed again. He was such a worrywart sometimes.

"I asked someone very persuasive to escort him here," she replied, fixing her top over the bandage to cover it.

"Did you make a friend?" he teased. He moved to the opposite side of the room where he leant back against the far wall and folded his arms over his broad chest. "I didn't think that was possible."

"I'm friends with you aren't I?" she said, raising a brow at him.

August laughed playfully. "We're more like dysfunctional siblings."

A wide grin spread on Nora's face, scrunching the sides of her eyes. "Okay, fair point."

The sound of muffled voices came from the hallway, followed by a quick succession of three taps. August pulled the door open abruptly, surprising those on the other side. Lord Porcella didn't get a chance to utter a single protest or move away before August dragged him in by his collar. Cole stared at Nora, his gaze running over her front. Judging by the look in his eyes, the bloodstain would definitely not pass as a pattern in the fabric.

"Wh—" Cole didn't get to finish his sentence. August hit him over the head, rendering him unconscious in one swift blow. He caught Cole in his arms before he could hit the hallway floor.

"What is the meaning of this?" Lord Porcella exclaimed, his panicked eyes darting around the room as his hands trembled at his sides. "What have you done?"

August was unbothered by the man's terror, kicking the door shut with his foot and unceremoniously dumping Cole's sleeping form on the floor in the office. Nora felt a little guilty. She liked the man, and he was *very* talented in the bedroom. Not to mention he'd been doing her a favour. She'd leave a few extra golden coins than she'd promised in his pockets and hopefully he wouldn't be too angry.

Sitting on the edge of the desk, she focused on the task at hand. Nora placed a hand over her heart, schooling a look of worry on her features. "What have we done? My lord, we came in here after hearing an awful noise to find you over that poor man!" She pointed to where the fake Robert Swiften lay. "The wild look in your eyes was like nothing I had ever seen before! What will your wife think of what you've done? Your son? You killed a man!"

"What? I—" he spluttered, his eyes going to the dead body on the floor. His skin paled and he swayed on the spot. Nora wondered whether he was going to pass out. She hoped not; she hated when things dragged out longer than they needed to. "Robert…"

"Was that his name?" Nora gasped, coming to stand beside Lord Porcella. She placed a gentle hand on his shoulder. "Isn't he beloved by the people? I saw how popular he was with the other nobles."

Lord Porcella's voice was barely audible, if she hadn't been so close to him she doubted she'd have heard his words. "You killed him."

Nora tsked. "No, you did this and there wasn't just us that saw you. There were others that witnessed you entering this room with him, of hearing that man's screams."

Lord Porcella trembled beneath her hand. He knew that even if what she was saying was false, that with a little coin and gossip, Nora's lies could easily become the truth.

"It was the right decision to make," August said from behind Lord Porcella, his voice low and reassuring. "He was, after all, disobeying King Dominic's laws. You did warn him. Gave him more courtesy than he was due. Executing him was the final straw."

Nora nodded. "You had to put the people's safety first. You were protecting your citizens."

"Are you threatening me?" Lord Porcella asked, narrowing his eyes. He made to raise his hands, but Nora stepped in front of him and placed hers gently over them. She slowly lowered his hands before he could think to summon his water magic.

"We are helping you," Nora replied, smiling sweetly as though they were kind strangers offering to assist him to paint a fence or carry a heavy load. "Helping you to win back King Dominic's favour and rid yourself of an evil man that had you by the balls. You should really be on your knees thanking us."

"Thank you?" He spluttered, panicked. "I am ruined. You have no idea what you've done."

Nora pouted her lips. "I'm sad you think so lowly of us and of yourself for that matter. You're a politician, are you not? It's all about spin and we have the perfect story for you."

"No story will get Robert Swiften Senior to see me favourably after the death of his son," Lord Porcella sighed, his shoulders slackening in defeat. This man was truly pathetic. "The Swiften family is powerful in Ocean's Harbour."

"Maybe," Nora shrugged nonchalantly. "But I have seen how the people see you, both the nobles and commoners. You are loved."

To Nora's pleasant surprise, Lord Porcella smiled at her words. It was small and fleeting, but it had happened, nonetheless.

"Agree to our terms and the Swiften family's power matter," August replied, offering him the metal tube Rana had given them. They weren't supposed to give it to the lord until he had agreed to their demands, but she wasn't going to call August out with an audience. "Agree, and the Swiften family will never be an issue for you again and you won't have to share your people's favour with anyone anymore. They will only look to you."

"And King Dominic, of course," Nora added, glancing at her friend.

"Of course," August repeated, and she could swear she heard him smile - if such a thing were even possible.

Lord Porcella untwisted the cap, drawing out the papers with King Dominic's seal. It was a collection of forged documents with witness reports and other evidence detailing the Robert Swiften and the rest of his family as human traffickers, labelling them responsible for the deaths of countless innocents.

"What is this?" He asked, his gaze scanning over the papers as he flicked through them.

"It's your job as the lord of Ocean Harbour to protect the people. Seems to me you were safeguarding citizens from being exploited by Robert Swiften and his entire family," Nora replied, stepping closer to the lord. He looked up at her, his gaze assessing as he tried to decide his next move. "King Dominic will answer your call for aid and support you in your valiant endeavour to rid Ocean's Harbour of such corruption."

Lord Porcella's brows furrowed but he nodded, sliding the documents back into the tube. "King Dominic is a just ruler. I am grateful for his support in this difficult time. Robert Swiften was a traitor and was executed as such. He was found in my office, attempting to steal private documents that would have put my citizens in danger, I had no choice but to end his life instantly. His family will be investigated for the role they play in the following days so that they too will be brought to justice."

Nora smiled wickedly. "Exactly."

"We'd advise sending correspondence to the king tonight," August said, moving to the door. "An avian Anima would reach Royal Bay in a day or so I would think. It's better to have King Dominic's support before Robert Swiften Senior can attempt to cause a scene. Wouldn't want to upset the people with his lies."

"Of course," Lord Porcella replied with a resigned look. The man had accepted his fate. For a man that captivated those around him, he was so very easily manipulated himself.

"Oh, and your son will be leaving for Royal Bay in the morning," August added. "King Dominic has graciously offered to be his steward. It is an honour that many would die for."

Lord Porcella begrudgingly nodded. "Of course. It would be a privilege."

Nora strode towards the door, pausing at the threshold to smile smugly at the lord. "Have a wonderful evening Lord Porcella. Your party was spectacular. I do hope we can attend another soon."

7

After retrieving more appropriate attire, Nora found herself sitting on the wall bordering Robert Swiften's home. It was closer to the harbour than Lord Porcella's estate—only a few streets back from the water. His property wasn't what Nora was expecting. It wasn't grand or ostentatious like so many nobles in Royal Bay liked their homes to be. Instead, it had a modesty about it, which was ideal as the smaller grounds were easier to observe and navigate.

"They're all sound asleep," August declared, coming to sit by Nora and sliding off his hood. She glanced around, spotting one of the guards he had rendered unconscious in a garden bed.

"Perfect," Nora whispered, turning her head to face him. "Put your hood back on. We should move now before he notices that he's no longer protected."

August shook his head, the moonlight catching his dirty blond hair and his pointed ears that peaked out between the strands. It was starting to get long, now extending beyond its usual inch from his scalp. "Not yet."

Nora frowned. "Why? What are—"

"Robbie!" A woman's voice called, and Nora turned her head to see the familiar face from that evening. It was the woman who had been chasing the fake Robert Swiften around the festivities back at Lord Porcella's estate. "Robbie, open up!"

She stumbled up the steps then proceeded to bang her fist on the front door. She hadn't noticed the guard who lay unconscious only a few feet away, her attention fixed on her desperation to see Robert Swiften. A dim light became visible as it moved through the house towards the ruckus at the front. The woman made to pound her fist again when the door swung open, and her hand collided with Robert's face. He cried out, dropping the lamp he'd been holding to the steps where it shattered and extinguished the light.

Luckily, the skies were clear, and the moon above provided enough light that the duo was still visible. Nora and August watched as Robert clutched his face and the woman waved her hands around in a panic.

"Oh, Robbie! I'm so sorry!"

"Holly!" Robert replied, his voice coming out nasally thanks to his hold on his nose. "What are you doing here?"

"I had to see you! I had to tell you that I don't care that you slept with that woman!" She exclaimed. Nora smirked, knowing full well who the woman was talking about. "We can still be together."

"What woman? What—" Robert stopped speaking abruptly, his shoulders going rigid, then hastily added. "Holly you need to go. Go home."

"But Robbie!"

"Go home, Holly!" Robert shut the door in the woman's face and Nora may have felt a little bad for her, but that was short-lived as Holly began to wail like a creature from legendary stories that were written to scare children.

"I can't believe you stole her boyfriend," August teased under his breath as Holly slowly stumbled back down the path away from the house, her sobs shaking her slumped shoulders.

"I can't steal anything from her that she never owned in the first place," Nora replied with a wink. "And I didn't sleep with him." She made a gagging motion, sticking out her tongue which earned her a chuckle from August. "Come on, let's go."

Pulling his hood up, August dropped to the ground and Nora followed after. Their feet made no sound as they hit the dirt and crept towards a side door where August knelt to pick the lock. It took him only seconds before the lock clicked and they let themselves in. The house was dark—no candles or oil lamps lit to provide any light—and the scent of lavender lingered in the air. August led the way upstairs to where a warm glow came from the room at the far end of the hallway.

Tiptoeing on silent feet, Nora flexed her fingers, readying to summon her magic. They neared the door and August edged it open only to find the bedroom deserted.

"Where the fuck is he?" Nora hissed beneath her breath, her eyes flickering over the room for Robert Swiften.

The sound of a door slamming downstairs had them spinning on their heels and running out of the room.

"He must have seen one of the sentries passed out!" August shouted as they pounded down the floorboards in pursuit. August leapt over the railing, landing on the lower floor with a loud thud as Nora slid down the bannister of the staircase.

That was why he'd froze and stumbled over his words, Nora thought. The man's paranoia had helped him escape their grasp, but not for long. His running would only delay the inevitable. Robert Swiften was already racing out across the garden by the time they reached the back doors, but the small lead he had didn't bother Nora. There was something thrilling about the chase. The man looked over his shoulder with wide eyes and threw a dagger in their direction.

Nora quickly flicked her wrists, putting up an air shield to block the weapon from hitting either her or August then threw a series of pebble-sized fireballs at Robert in quick succession. He yelped like a kicked dog before scurrying through the gate and out onto the street.

He led them towards the harbour where there were very few people around. Those that were remained at the far end of the dock watching as a large ship sailed away in the distance. Robert ran in the opposite direction towards a cluster of smaller boats tied to the dock by ropes. Was he planning to sail away?

He sprinted towards the edge of the deck, grappling with one of the knots binding the last boat. Nora cornered him, throwing fireballs into each of the boats and setting them ablaze. There was no place to go now but through her. Robert's head snapped back and forth, his golden curls illuminated by the flames bouncing around his cheeks as he looked between her and the burning boats.

"Wait!" he begged, his hands raised in defeat.

"Why?" she rebuked, eyeing him like prey. "So you can help more criminals?"

He frowned, blood from where Holly had hit him crusted under his nose as he shook his head slowly. "Is it a crime to want to be free?"

"It is if you're trying to escape a punishment or are going against the laws of the king," Nora said, putting her hands on her hip. Criminals had no right to freedom.

"And what if you are being punished for purely existing?" he asked. "What if the king's laws weren't made for everyone? You are blinded by your privilege."

"Ha! That's rich coming from one of the wealthiest men in the southern cities. And to top it off, you have the balls to think I'm privileged!" Nora laughed. It was a ridiculous statement. She had no money, no social standing, absolutely nothing to her name. As far as society was concerned, being an Alta meant that she didn't even exist.

"With an Elementum king, this country is made for you. His laws serve to benefit you."

Nora couldn't believe the lies he was spouting. Every citizen had to follow the laws in Valmenessia, there was no buffet to pick more favourable ones. Every law was to be adhered to by every citizen. With ideals like this, Nora could see why Robert Swiften was a danger to Valmenessia. King Dominic was right; this man had to be stopped.

"The king's laws benefit all."

The man looked over her shoulder. "Are you so sure about that?"

Nora turned to where August stood behind her, his face lit by the light of the fires, watching their interaction. His hood must have fallen back in his effort to catch up. The planes of his strong nose and pointed ears, his chiselled jawline and the dark pools of his eyes were visible for her and Robert to see. She frowned but turned back at the sound of splashing water. To her surprise, Robert had launched himself into the water and was swimming towards the departing ship in the distance. Had he lost his mind? There was no way any sane Anima—or anyone with magic, for that matter—would try to leave Valmenessia. It was a sacrifice too huge to contemplate.

She summoned her water magic, dragging him back to the dock through a vortex and throwing him onto the wooden planks. "Don't be an idiot."

Robert coughed, but didn't rise from the ground, instead opting to look like a drowned rat. He shivered, his fear evident in his eyes. "Since when is trying to save one's life stupidity?"

"It wouldn't be if there was a possibility of success, but you are just delaying the inevitable," August said, coming to stand by Nora as she summoned the water from his clothing, the liquid seeping from the fabric and dripping through the boards to the sea below. "It's sad, really. I would have thought you'd at least attempt to shift, but maybe deep down you know this is the end for you. Although I still would have enjoyed watching a sloth try to run away from us."

Nora laughed at August's revelation of Robert Swiften's shift; a sloth wasn't exactly advantageous in an escape attempt.

"This doesn't have to be inevitable," Robert begged, his voice wavering in his desperation. "You could let me live."

Nora tsked. "But you're already dead. You even handed us the decoy body we needed to prove how you were executed by Lord Porcella for your crimes." Nora gestured with her hand at him. "All we are doing now is tidying up loose ends."

Without waiting for his reply, she flicked her wrists, lighting him up in flames. His arms flailed as he rolled in desperation to put out the fire. Robert screamed as Nora pushed more heat into the flames that were desperate to devour him. The air filled with the scent of burning flesh as the fiery boats grew brighter as they, too, fed off her magic. Nora felt nothing than resolve as she watched the man die. The king wanted him dead so she couldn't let him live. If Robert had escaped—even to another country—he would remain a threat and could easily spread his ideals or choose to return without his magic. After all, you didn't need magic to change the way the world spun. Belief was the most powerful force. Not only did it have the power to alter the direction of the world but it was able to remake it entirely. The king commanded Robert Swiften's death and Nora did not falter. She was the sword in his hand; sharp and deadly.

August placed a hand on Nora's shoulder and they both waited in silence for Robert Swiften's body to blacken before turning to ash. As the sun slowly rose in the sky, Nora summoned her wind magic, blowing his remains into the sea breeze.

"Time to go," August said, tugging on his hood and turning away from the blackened patch on the boards.

Nora nodded, following her friend away from the dock. "Let's go home."

8

Nora and August travelled north by horseback to Royal
Bay. They hadn't bothered waiting around to see
whether Lord Porcella made good on his promise to
follow through with King Dominic's demands. They would hear
about it soon enough—gossip spread quicker than a disease. Nora
was eager to return home and notify Rana and the king of their
success. Nothing compared to the rush she got from declaring a
job complete. Fortunately, they were half a day's ride from the
capital city of Valmenessia, so she would not have to wait much
longer.

August pulled his horse to a stop at the side of the road and
Nora slowed to meet him. They had taken one of the quieter
routes through farmland and orchards, so there weren't many
people around. It was safer that way, with less eyes on August's
hooded form and more opportunities for him to remove it should
the weather get too hot.

"There looks to be a farmhouse over there," he said, pointing in the distance.

"I'll get us something to eat," she offered, handing August the reins to her horse. "I won't be long."

Dismounting, Nora left August with the horses and made her way up the path between the tall grass. Cows and sheep grazed in the paddocks and, behind the farmhouse, trees grew in rows. Nora strode towards a simple stall that was set up outside the front of the farmhouse, and as she drew closer, a girl a few years younger than Nora looked up from her needlework, a smile spreading on her round face.

"We have some delicious cheese and sweet apples for sale today," the girl said, picking up a round red fruit. She rose, giving Nora a glimpse of her simple dress. The pale blue fabric was faded and had mismatched buttons running down the front, and patches were sewn over her elbows. The girl extended her hand, presenting the apple to Nora. "Some of the best this season."

"I'll bet," Nora replied, offering her own smile before taking the apple and sniffing it. The sweet smell made her mouth water. "I'll take four and some cheese too. Have you had many visitors come by?"

The girl nodded as she packed Nora's purchases into a thin strip of cream-coloured fabric. "We've had a few."

"Did they tell you any juicy gossip?" Nora gave the girl a knowing look. "I bet you hear all sorts of things from passing travellers."

The girl blushed, the rich colour pretty on her sun-kissed skin. "I hear a bit."

Perfect.

Nora waited for the girl to elaborate, resting her hip on the side of the stall and folding her arms over her chest. She took a bite of the apple she still held, its juices running down her chin.

"Rumours have been circling that the Southern Wolf Pack is leaving."

That was odd. There were two main wolf packs in

Valmenessia—the Southern and Northern—and both were tight-knit communities of Anima with deep roots in the territories they'd claimed. The packs were known for moving around, but to leave altogether? That was unusual. Nora wondered what would cause the Southern Wolf Pack to up and leave not only their territory but their history and traditions that were tied to the area. Perhaps the wolf packs were merging, but why would they create one large pack? As far as Nora knew, they didn't always get along.

Nora raised a brow and said through a mouthful. "Really? Are they joining their kin in the north?"

"I don't know," the girl shrugged, her black ponytail swaying with the movement. "They have to go somewhere, don't they? They can't just disappear."

"That would take a lot of magic," Nora agreed.

"We usually get a few members from the pack come through here, but Mama said they won't be coming this way anymore."

"Maybe they just don't like your produce?" Nora teased, grinning mischievously.

Cheeks reddening, the girl frowned at Nora.

"It was only a joke," Nora quickly said, raising her hands in placation, the apple pinched between her thumb and finger. "This is the best apple I've ever eaten." She took another bite. "I swear to the Goddess Thyra."

The girl's eyebrows shot up, her hands stilling before her. She spoke in a rushed whisper, "You shouldn't swear on the Gods and Goddesses."

"But how would you know that I was telling you the truth then?"

"You should cross your heart or something," the girl replied, showing Nora the action by drawing a cross over her own chest. "I don't care what you do, but you should never talk about the Gods and Goddesses like that."

"Okay," Nora grinned. "I'll do that next time."

"Good," the girl said, offering Nora the bundle of food. "The wolf pack aren't the only ones leaving. Apparently Lord Porcella's son, Blaine, is going to live in Royal Bay with King Dominic." She looked up at Nora expectantly, curling the end of her ponytail between her fingers. "Do you think he'll meet the princes? I hear they are really handsome."

Nora laughed. It was true, the princes were very attractive. She'd seen them in passing, but she was forbidden to speak to them, let alone alert them to her presence. Like the rest of Valmenessia, they didn't know about the Alta. "I'd hazard a guess and say that he will."

"Wow," the girl replied in awe, clasping her hands in front of her. "I hope one day I can go to Royal Bay. I'd never get to meet a prince but maybe I could see one."

"You never know what the future holds," Nora winked, handing the girl a few gold coins. "Thank you for the food and the gossip, too."

The girl's green eyes widened at the hefty sum of money now resting in her hand. "Did you steal this?"

Nora chuckled. "No."

"How do you have so much coin? *Who* are you?"

Nora smiled at the girl. "I'm no one."

It wasn't a lie, at least as far as the citizens of Valmenessian were concerned.

Nora was an Alta, which is to say, she did not exist.

THE STORY CONTINUES...

Find out what happens to Nora in Liars and Light, Book One of the Valmenessian Chronicles.

THE VALMENESSIAN CHRONICLES

Alta: A Valmenessian Novella

Liars and Light

Rise and Reverence

Maker: A Valmenessian Novella

Vice and Verity

Also By Rebecca

The Terrulian Trials
By Chloe Hodge and Rebecca Camm

A Sky of Storms

A Forest of Fire

A Sea of Secrets

A City of Smoke

A Desert of Despair

A Kingdom of Conquerors

I'm a daughter of House Jupiter, the empire's most powerful family built on the backs of those brainwashed to serve.

The king is dead, and the Terrulian Trials have begun. This is my one chance to be crowned ruler of the kingdom and right my family's wrongs.

If only it were that simple.

The House of Ascension isn't for the fainthearted. I must survive three deadly challenges to secure my place as queen—and that's not counting the Potentials ready to stab me in the back.

It doesn't help that four sinfully good-looking guys keep messing with my head. I can't trust anyone, least of all myself.

There can only be one sovereign … and I'll stop at nothing to win these vicious games.

The Terrulian Trials is a steamy urban fantasy series brimming with mystery, magic, and blood. This is a "why choose" novel, meaning the heroine ends up with multiple love interests. This novel is recommended for readers 18+ and is book one of six.

About The Author

Rebecca Camm was raised in Melbourne by a single mother who encouraged her passion for reading and all things magical. She has been writing stories since she was a child to help manage her anxiety and make sense of the world.

Rebecca strongly believes in the power stories have in changing lives. Just like her, Rebecca's characters are flawed, yet they are continually learning. Unlike her, they are confident, witty, and just generally more exciting.

Rebecca lives with her husband and two children. When her children allow her free time, she is either writing or attempting to conquer her ever-growing tbr pile.

Stay in touch!

Website rebeccacamm.com

Newsletter rebeccacamm.com/contact

Instagram @readingwritingdaydreaming

TikTok @readingwritingdaydream

Facebook @readingwritingdaydreaming

Facebook Group facebook.com/groups/rebeccacammsreadergroup